A Giant First-Start Reader

This easy reader contains only 53 different words,
repeated often to help the young reader develop
word recognition and interest in reading.

Basic word list for *Busy Bunnies*

a	here	sleepy
and	in	spring
bunnies	is	sunny
busy	it	that
cheep	Leo	the
Cleo	little	there
dig	make	things
do	new	time
dream	of	to
eat	on	two
eyes	*peep*	under
garden	Robbie	up
go	rubs	wake
goes	says	water
good	seeds	we
grass	sees	what
green	sky	will
grow		yes

Busy Bunnies

Written by Stephen Caitlin

Illustrated by Ben Mahan

Troll Associates

Library of Congress Cataloging in Publication Data

Caitlin, Stephen.
  Busy bunnies.

    Summary: Bunnies Leo and Cleo welcome the coming
of spring by working in their garden and thinking
of all the good things to eat they are going to
grow.
    [1. Rabbits—Fiction. 2. Spring—Fiction.
3. Gardening—Fiction] I. Mahan, Ben, ill. II. Title.
PZ7.Cl22Bu   1988   [E]   87-10912
ISBN 0-8167-1083-X (lib. bdg.)
ISBN 0-8167-1084-8 (pbk.)

Cheep-peep!
Wake up!

"What is that?" says Leo.

"What is that?" says Cleo.

Leo rubs two sleepy eyes.
Leo sees the sunny sky.

Cleo rubs two sleepy eyes.
Cleo sees the new green grass.

"Yes," says Cleo to Leo.
"It is spring!"

"*Cheep-peep,*" says Robbie.
"Spring is a busy time."

Leo is busy under the sunny sky.

Cleo is busy in the new green grass.

What will the busy bunnies make?
"We will make a garden!" says Leo.
"We will grow good things to eat."

What busy bunnies!
Dig, dig, dig . . .
a little here,
a little there.

In go the seeds . . .
a little here,
a little there.

And on goes the water . . .
a little here,
a little there.

"There," says Leo to Cleo.
"What a good garden!"

"Yes," says Cleo to Leo.
"We will grow good things to eat!"

There goes Leo,
under the sunny sky.

There goes Cleo
in the new green grass.

What sleepy bunnies!
What do sleepy bunnies dream
of in the spring?

A garden of good things to eat!